First Published by Ink Gladiators Press®

Translations Of Hope

Editor-in-Chief: Reena Doss

First Edition
ISBN 13: 978-93-49117-82-2

Castle Secrets For You—Lantern 3

Credits:
Book Design by Leonie Belle Hawk
German & Romanian Translations: Edited and Proofed by Justin Adam Wolf and Aelius Arche

Ink Gladiators Press®
Publishing and promoting warriors on life's battlefield
Founded in 2019 | Bangalore, India
www.inkgladiatorspress.com

To my beloved Weaver,

who has given me the most beautiful gifts that I am still discovering;
this is my wholehearted thanksgiving to you for giving my voice
meaning, imagery, and wonder everytime I create from it

To my future family,

the ones all of this is for; may we keep encouraging each other
to have faith, trust in the Weaver and believe in His love,
especially when the roads ahead feel uncertain

To my dear Sisters,

who listened avidly to all my first made up stories,
dolls we set up and art sketches I painted to give you a theatre;
may imagination, fantasy and dreaming be something
you keep close for yourself and for your children

This book is a lantern of
Castle Secrets For You

Love Adores
Never-ending Tales:
Eagerly Ready, News Sails

The main content is written in English,
with German and Romanian translations
added after each piece.

Castles Secrets For You

Because Mental Health Matters

I stopped numbering my pages because my story is still being written.

Besides, I do like its symbol a lot—a sleeping 8.

I'll find you in the dark because I'm the girl

who loves to stay *lost* amongst the midnight stars

caught up with moonbeams *in a lantern*

trying to find my way back *home*

Lanterns

The pleasure of watching light move across the night sky against its deep purples, blues and greys is an incredible sight to behold.

Though I have never seen it in person myself except on TV, reels or videos, I would imagine that it mimics the feeling of a thousand golden suns glimmering brighter than the stars behind them. I would imagine that it would capture the feeling of remembering that we are each important because no matter how small or big we are light travels faster than sound. I would imagine it would make anyone who sees them smile, open their hearts as hope flutters like birdsong near their door, and the taste of something indescribably good wraps them warmly.

Lanterns are necessary because igniting hope is the best cure in support of mental health awareness. Many live in darkness, in a state of feeling disillusioned by those they put their faith in and have forgotten how to see their own hearts through eyes that love, but a lantern is meant for just this purpose—to relight someone's candle with kindness, to hold a hand steadily in their shadows, and to listen gently to the broken pieces in others speaking. Sometimes, the truth is simple.

That delicate point between human nature and the desire to do what is good is where we will meet the Author of Love. Love can only be known from the One who created us and even when people (who follow God) make us feel like He isn't real or there for us, one of the best ways to reconnect with Him directly is to love with all your heart—and to balance it with healthy discernment, boundaries and truth in situations where your broken parts might want to do, feel or say the exact opposite. *E.g.: Jesus Christ*

It is my joy to let go of this lantern—as all lanterns must be—for others to find because I want to share something beautiful that I gained and that is mine to offer: You are deeply loved by Heavenly Hands that have constructed, created and command time, space, and distance.

Forest King

Once upon a time, in a faraway kingdom, there lived a grand King who was loved by all creative people.

He was well known for his support of literature, art, and performances rather than war, like other kings. He always wore a white uniform with a gold belt, a blue rose brooch, and twin violet bows on his boots. His crown had engraved motifs of a lion, a swan, and a wolf. Though he was popular with his subjects and court officials, he was called "a mystery." No one quite knew what he did in his private time, for he was not married, nor did anyone have anything ill to say about him.

But if you asked him—as the time-travelling sparrow did and told me later—it was because he was busy wearing a mask and performing at the local opera house. How did he get there, you might ask? Well, he had a secret entrance from the woods behind his house to the backstage door of the theatre. No soul in the kingdom knew they had been clapping for the Forest King.

Inspired by Neuschwanstein Castle, Germany

Waldkönig

Es war einmal in einem weit entfernten Königreich ein großer König, der von allen kreativen Menschen geliebt wurde.

Er war bekannt dafür, dass er Literatur, Kunst und Darstellende Künste förderte, anstatt wie andere Könige Krieg zu führen. Er trug immer eine weiße Uniform mit einem goldenen Gürtel, einer blauen Rosenbrosche und zwei violetten Schleifen an seinen Stiefeln. Auf seiner Krone waren Motive eines Löwen, eines Schwans und eines Wolfes eingraviert. Obwohl er bei seinen Untertanen und Hofbeamten beliebt war, wurde er als „Rätsel" bezeichnet. Niemand wusste genau, was er in seiner Freizeit tat, denn er war nicht verheiratet, und niemand hatte etwas Schlechtes über ihn zu sagen.

Aber wenn man ihn fragte—wie es der zeitreisende Spatz tat und mir später erzählte –, dann lag das daran, dass er damit beschäftigt war, eine Maske zu tragen und im örtlichen Opernhaus aufzutreten. Wie er dorthin kam, fragen Sie sich vielleicht? Nun, er hatte einen geheimen Zugang vom Wald hinter seinem Haus zur Hintertür des Theaters. Niemand im Königreich wusste, dass sie dem Waldkönig applaudiert hatten.

Inspiriert vom Schloss Neuschwanstein, Deutschland

Regele Pădurii

A fost odată, într-un regat îndepărtat, un mare rege care era iubit de toţi oamenii creativi.

Era cunoscut pentru sprijinul acordat literaturii, artei şi spectacolelor, spre deosebire de alţi regi, care se concentrau mai degrabă pe război. Purta întotdeauna o uniformă albă cu o centură aurie, o broşă cu trandafir albastru şi două funde violete pe cizme. Coroana lui avea gravate motive cu un leu, un lebăd şi un lup. Deşi era popular printre supuşii şi oficialii curţii, era numit „un mister". Nimeni nu ştia cu exactitate ce făcea în timpul liber, pentru că nu era căsătorit şi nimeni nu avea nimic rău de spus despre el.

Dar dacă l-ai fi întrebat—aşa cum a făcut-o vrabia călătoare în timp şi mi-a povestit mai târziu—era pentru că era ocupat să poarte o mască şi să joace la opera locală. Cum ajungea acolo, te-ai putea întreba? Ei bine, avea o intrare secretă din pădurea din spatele casei sale către uşa din culise a teatrului. Niciun suflet din regat nu ştia că aplaudau Regele Pădurii.

Inspirat de Castelul Neuschwanstein, Germania

Bear's Truth

Once upon a time, there was a giant fortress situated on the highest rocks you can imagine possible. It was more imposing because its gray stone was painted over in pure white, which made people wonder who oversaw the design, structure, and maintenance. No one knew, for even the eagles dared not nest there.

It first belonged to a retired pirate who made his home there. Not much is known about him except that he was falsely accused of a crime, but when the executioners tried to drown his entire household, it is said that a large wave took them far away. Later, the fortress served as the King's military base to protect the land from invasion. But because their kingdom was mostly peaceful, war turned inward.

When the King's only daughter fell in love and ran away with a poor soldier named Bear, the King was furious. An ambitious courtier, who had planned to marry his own son to the Princess, seized the opportunity to successfully twist the King's mind with venom. Then began the most cruel trials of the century.

Any person who could not pay a certain amount to the crown was called a practising wizard or witch. If a parent couldn't afford the sum, the children were not spared either. Once a place of protection, the fortress became a state prison. Trials were held every month, and anyone found guilty was thrown over the highest rock and left to drown in the sea.

When the Princess heard what was happening in her kingdom, she returned with Bear on a silver horse. She rode into the fortress, stood in front of her father and his greedy court, stared at each one in turn, before she directed the horse to face the rocks.

Then, in one swift moment, just as the horse leaped, she breathed words that couldn't be heard and held Bear with a smile as they fell into the great seas.

However, the villagers believe that it was impossible for them to die, because many swore they saw every innocent transform into merfolk.

Inspired by Hohenwerfen Castle, Austria

Die Wahrheit des Bären

Es war einmal eine riesige Festung, die auf den höchsten Felsen stand, die man sich vorstellen kann. Sie wirkte noch imposanter, weil ihr grauer Stein in reinem Weiß gestrichen war, was die Menschen dazu veranlasste, sich zu fragen, wer für die Gestaltung, den Bau und die Instandhaltung verantwortlich war. Niemand wusste es, denn selbst die Adler wagten es nicht, dort zu nisten.

Zuerst gehörte sie einem pensionierten Piraten, der sich dort niedergelassen hatte. Über ihn ist nicht viel bekannt, außer dass er zu Unrecht eines Verbrechens beschuldigt wurde. Als die Henker versuchten, seine gesamte Familie zu ertränken, soll eine große Welle sie weit weggetragen haben. Später diente die Festung als Militärbasis des Königs, um das Land vor Invasionen zu schützen. Da ihr Königreich jedoch größtenteils friedlich war, wandte sich der Krieg nach innen.

Als sich die einzige Tochter des Königs verliebte und mit einem armen Soldaten namens Bär durchbrannte, war der König außer sich vor Wut.

Ein ehrgeiziger Höfling, der geplant hatte, seinen eigenen Sohn mit der Prinzessin zu verheiraten, nutzte die Gelegenheit, um den König mit giftigen Worten erfolgreich zu verwirren. Dann begannen die grausamsten Prozesse des Jahrhunderts.

Jeder, der nicht einen bestimmten Betrag an die Krone zahlen konnte, wurde als praktizierender Zauberer oder Hexe bezeichnet. Wenn Eltern sich die Summe nicht leisten konnten, wurden auch die Kinder nicht verschont. Die Festung, einst ein Ort des Schutzes, wurde zu einem Staatsgefängnis.

Jeden Monat fanden Prozesse statt, und jeder, der für schuldig befunden wurde, wurde über den höchsten Felsen geworfen und dem Ertrinken im Meer überlassen.

Als die Prinzessin hörte, was in ihrem Königreich vor sich ging, kehrte sie mit Bear auf einem silbernen Pferd zurück. Sie ritt in die Festung, stellte sich vor ihren Vater und seinen gierigen Hofstaat, starrte jeden einzelnen an, bevor sie das Pferd auf die Felsen zusteuerte.

Dann, in einem einzigen schnellen Moment, gerade als das Pferd sprang, flüsterte sie unhörbare Worte und hielt Bären mit einem Lächeln fest, während sie in die weite See stürzten.

Die Dorfbewohner glauben jedoch, dass es unmöglich war, dass sie starben, denn viele schworen, dass sie gesehen hätten, wie sich alle Unschuldigen in Meerjungfrauen verwandelten.

Inspiriert von der Burg Hohenwerfen in Österreich

Adevărul Ursului

A fost odată ca niciodată o fortăreață uriașă situată pe cele mai înalte stânci pe care vi le puteți imagina. Era și mai impunătoare deoarece piatra sa cenușie era vopsită în alb pur, ceea ce îi făcea pe oameni să se întrebe cine supraveghea proiectarea, structura și întreținerea ei. Nimeni nu știa, pentru că nici măcar vulturii nu îndrăzneau să-și facă cuiburi acolo.

A aparținut inițial unui pirat pensionat care și-a făcut acolo casa. Nu se știu multe despre el, cu excepția faptului că a fost acuzat pe nedrept de o crimă, dar când călăii au încercat să-i înece întreaga familie, se spune că un val mare i-a dus departe. Mai târziu, fortăreața a servit ca bază militară a regelui pentru a proteja țara de invazie. Dar, deoarece regatul lor era în mare parte pașnic, războiul s-a îndreptat spre interior.

Când singura fiică a regelui s-a îndrăgostit și a fugit cu un soldat sărac pe nume Urs, regele a fost furios. Un curtean ambițios, care plănuise să-și căsătorească propriul fiu cu prințesa, a profitat de ocazie pentru a-i răsturna cu succes mintea regelui cu venin. Apoi au început cele mai crude procese ale secolului.

Orice persoană care nu putea plăti o anumită sumă coroanei era numită vrăjitor sau vrăjitoare practicantă. Dacă un părinte nu își putea permite suma, nici copiii nu erau cruțați. Odată un loc de protecție, fortăreața a devenit o închisoare de stat. Procesele aveau loc în fiecare lună, iar oricine era găsit vinovat era aruncat de pe cea mai înaltă stâncă și lăsat să se înece în mare.

Când prinţesa a auzit ce se întâmpla în regatul ei, s-a întors cu Bear pe un cal argintiu. A intrat în fortăreaţă, s-a aşezat în faţa tatălui ei şi a curţii sale lacome, i-a privit pe rând pe fiecare, apoi a îndreptat calul spre stânci.

Apoi, într-o clipă, chiar când calul a sărit, ea a şoptit cuvinte care nu puteau fi auzite şi l-a îmbrăţişat pe Urs cu un zâmbet, în timp ce cădeau în marea întinsă.

Cu toate acestea, sătenii cred că era imposibil ca ei să moară, deoarece mulţi au jurat că i-au văzut pe toţi cei nevinovaţi transformându-se în sirene.

Inspirat de Castelul Hohenwerfen, Austria

Aquamarine Monster

Once upon a time, on the edge of a coastal kingdom, there lived a monster. He was so frightening to look at that people said they couldn't move when he turned to stare at them. He was known to protect the land and its people as long as they did not interfere with him. He was seven feet tall, with aquamarine scales for skin. He had hands like a human, but he also had shark fins growing out of his back. His feet were webbed, and he carried many conch shells in a pouch.

Often, his silhouette would be seen sitting at the top of a high mountain peak, making a low yet resounding trumpeting sound with the hollow of his hands. When invaders would draw near, he would dive into the deep places where the land ended and the seas began to intercept them. Though the King had asked him to bring invaders to be tried in the kingdom, the monster had refused. Instead, he used his appearance to frighten them, and if they ever saw him as a challenge to conquer, they learned soon enough that no arrow, spear, or bullet could penetrate his skin. Terror would then be visible on their faces as the monster laughed openly at their fragile attempts to put distance between him and their ideas of normal.

Why he chose to protect this particular kingdom when he obeyed no king was never known. His existence was simply accepted, for he had been known to be around for a few centuries. Only a pod of dolphins that had stayed close to his trumpeting song of comfort throughout their generations knew the legend of the man who was no monster.

Inspired by Palácio da Pena, Portugal

Das Aquamarin-Monster

Es war einmal ein Monster, das am Rande eines Küstenkönigreichs lebte. Es sah so furchterregend aus, dass die Menschen sagten, sie könnten sich nicht mehr bewegen, wenn es sich zu ihnen umdrehte und sie anstarrte. Es war bekannt dafür, das Land und seine Bewohner zu beschützen, solange sie sich nicht in seine Angelegenheiten einmischten.

Es war über zwei Meter groß und hatte eine Haut aus aquamarinfarbenen Schuppen. Es hatte Hände wie ein Mensch, aber aus seinem Rücken wuchsen Haifischflossen. Seine Füße waren mit Schwimmhäuten versehen, und er trug viele Muschelschalen in einem Beutel mit sich.

Oft sah man seine Silhouette auf dem Gipfel eines hohen Berges sitzen, wo er mit seinen hohlen Händen einen tiefen, aber hallenden Trompetenton erzeugte. Wenn sich Eindringlinge näherten, tauchte er in die Tiefen, wo das Land endete und das Meer begann, um sie abzufangen. Obwohl der König ihn gebeten hatte, die Eindringlinge zur Verurteilung ins Königreich zu bringen, lehnte das Monster dies ab. Stattdessen nutzte es sein Aussehen, um ihnen Angst einzujagen, und wenn sie es jemals als Herausforderung betrachteten, es zu besiegen, lernten sie schnell, dass kein Pfeil, Speer oder Kugel seine Haut durchdringen konnte. Dann war der Schrecken in ihren Gesichtern zu sehen, während das Monster offen über ihre kläglichen Versuche lachte, ihn von ihrer Vorstellung von Normalität fernzuhalten.

Warum er sich entschied, gerade dieses Königreich zu beschützen, obwohl er keinem König gehorchte, wurde nie bekannt. Seine Existenz wurde einfach akzeptiert, denn man wusste, dass es ihn schon seit einigen Jahrhunderten gab.

Nur eine Gruppe von Delfinen, die über Generationen hinweg seinem beruhigenden Gesang nahe geblieben war, kannte die Legende des Mannes, der kein Monster war.

Inspiriert vom Palácio da Pena, Portugal

∞

Monstrul Aquamarine

A fost odată, la marginea unui regat de coastă, un monstru. Era atât de înfricoșător încât oamenii spuneau că nu se puteau mișca când se întorcea să-i privească. Era cunoscut pentru faptul că proteja pământul și oamenii atâta timp cât aceștia nu-l deranjau. Avea doi metri înălțime și pielea acoperită cu solzi de culoarea acvamarinului. Avea mâini ca ale unui om, dar și aripioare de rechin care îi creșteau din spate. Picioarele îi erau palmate și purta multe cochilii de melc într-o pungă.

Adesea, silueta lui era văzută așezată în vârful unui munte înalt, scoțând un sunet slab, dar răsunător, cu palmele. Când invadatorii se apropiau, el se scufunda în adâncurile unde se termina pământul și începea marea, pentru a-i intercepta. Deși regele îi ceruse să-i aducă pe invadatori pentru a fi judecați în regat, monstrul refuzase. În schimb, își folosea înfățișarea pentru a-i speria, iar dacă îl vedeau ca pe o provocare de cucerit, aflau destul de repede că nici o săgeată, suliță sau glonț nu îi putea penetra pielea. Teroarea se citea atunci pe fețele lor, în timp ce monstrul râdea deschis de încercările lor fragile de a-l distanța de ideile lor despre normalitate.

Nu s-a știut niciodată de ce a ales să protejeze acest regat anume, când el nu se supunea niciunui rege. Existența lui era pur și simplu acceptată, pentru că se știa că era prezent de câteva secole. Doar un grup de delfini care rămăseseră aproape de cântecul lui liniștitor de-a lungul generațiilor lor cunoșteau legenda omului care nu era un monstru.

Inspirat de Palácio da Pena, Portugalia

Treason's Curse

Once upon a time, there was a young prince who fell madly in love with a queen's lady-in-waiting. Overcome by his feelings and awaiting the king's permission to marry her, he threw himself into the arduous task of building her a castle by the sea, where they could simply be—raise a family and enjoy the beauty of their gardens growing. But this was not to be, for barely had they married when he was executed for treason.

One is not sure if this was true or not, but his wife went mad with grief and cursed the king, who had added it to his name on her death. She refused to stay in it and said that anyone who lived there and had a connection to his unjust death would die a violent death in a foreign land. As many people started to report the truth of this, the king feared for his reputation, and so, to deflect from this scrutiny, his courtiers started another rumour. They spread a story around a fact to confuse what they didn't know how to control. They said his brother had stolen a jinxed sphinx from Egypt, which was why he was already cursed.

The prince's ghost, however, is said to be seen wandering the castle grounds. And after his wife passed away, she too was heard calling his name when the winds were strong and the seas howled.

Inspired by Castello di Miramare, Italy

Der Fluch des Verrats

Es war einmal ein junger Prinz, der sich unsterblich in die Hofdame einer Königin verliebte. Überwältigt von seinen Gefühlen und in Erwartung der Erlaubnis des Königs, sie heiraten zu dürfen, stürzte er sich in die mühsame Aufgabe, ihr ein Schloss am Meer zu bauen, wo sie einfach nur sein konnten—eine Familie gründen und die Schönheit ihrer Gärten genießen. Doch daraus wurde nichts, denn kaum hatten sie geheiratet, wurde er wegen Verrats hingerichtet.

Man weiß nicht, ob dies wahr ist oder nicht, aber seine Frau wurde vor Kummer wahnsinnig und verfluchte den König, der dies ihrem Namen bei ihrem Tod hinzugefügt hatte. Sie weigerte sich, dort zu bleiben, und sagte, dass jeder, der dort lebte und mit seinem ungerechten Tod in Verbindung stand, einen gewaltsamen Tod in einem fremden Land sterben würde. Als viele Menschen begannen, die Wahrheit darüber zu berichten, fürchtete der König um seinen Ruf, und um von dieser Untersuchung abzulenken, verbreiteten seine Höflinge ein weiteres Gerücht. Sie verbreiteten eine Geschichte um eine Tatsache herum, um das zu verschleiern, was sie nicht kontrollieren konnten. Sie sagten, sein Bruder habe eine verfluchte Sphinx aus Ägypten gestohlen, weshalb er bereits verflucht sei.

Der Geist des Prinzen soll jedoch auf dem Schlossgelände umherwandern. Und nachdem seine Frau verstorben war, hörte man auch sie seinen Namen rufen, wenn der Wind stark wehte und die See heulte.

Inspiriert vom Castello di Miramare, Italien

Blestemul Trădării

A fost odată ca niciodată un tânăr prinț care s-a îndrăgostit nebunește de o doamnă de onoare a reginei. Copleșit de sentimentele sale și așteptând permisiunea regelui pentru a se căsători cu ea, s-a apucat de sarcina dificilă de a-i construi un castel lângă mare, unde ar fi putut pur și simplu să-și întemeieze o familie și să se bucure de frumusețea grădinilor lor înflorite. Dar acest lucru nu avea să se întâmple, pentru că abia se căsătoriseră când el a fost executat pentru trădare.

Nu se știe cu siguranță dacă acest lucru a fost adevărat sau nu, dar soția lui a înnebunit de durere și l-a blestemat pe rege, care i-a adăugat acest nume la al ei în momentul morții. Ea a refuzat să rămână acolo și a spus că oricine locuia acolo și avea o legătură cu moartea lui nedreaptă va muri violent într-o țară străină. Pe măsură ce tot mai mulți oameni au început să relateze adevărul, regele s-a temut pentru reputația sa și, pentru a distrage atenția de la această anchetă, curtenii săi au lansat un alt zvon. Au răspândit o poveste în jurul unui fapt pentru a confunda ceea ce nu știau cum să controleze. Au spus că fratele său furase un sfinx blestemat din Egipt, motiv pentru care era deja blestemat.

Cu toate acestea, se spune că fantoma prințului este văzută rătăcind pe terenul castelului. Și după ce soția sa a murit, și ea a fost auzită strigându-i numele când vântul bătea puternic și marea urla.

Inspirat de Castello di Miramare, Italia

Skeletons' Rust

Once upon a time, in a time not yet recorded, a lord built a wooden fortress, and there he stayed until he died. He was remembered as cruel, wicked, and uncommonly intelligent in such a way that even his enemies feared him.

In his youth, though, he had been of a different mettle—that is, until he fell in love. She was a peasant who sang at his family's functions. When his mother realized that he was falling in love with a commoner, she quickly arranged for the girl to be married in secret. But the girl was in love with the young lord and told him what had been decided by leaving a note on the bark of the tree they often visited to speak without ears. Furious, he told her to wait for him at the moon's starting hour. He then proceeded to confront his mother in a fit of his famous rage.

Fearing that her son would do something she did not approve of, she had him locked in a wine cellar. For days, he screamed, howled, and beat the door. When the staff pleaded with the mother to release him, she refused and said she would in a few months. Whispers spread in the manor that the young lord had lost his mind—and he had. With his bare hands, he began to dig a way out from under the cellar.

The girl, in the meantime, was married against her will. Believing her love had abandoned her, she stopped all the clocks in her new home at the time she and he had agreed to meet. When anyone tried to move them forward, she would become hysterical, so everyone left them as they were and hid their hand watches around her. Her new husband was not in love with her, and he saw no point in trying to find out what was wrong. He left her alone to wander by herself in the forest, believing she was mentally unstable.

Then one day, the young lord's mother passed away during a particularly stormy night. When the staff opened the cellar to inform their lord, they found a calm and composed young man sitting before them. He refused to see his mother's body and wished the funeral to be over and done with. This was not unexpected, given that everyone knew what his mother had done. Once this was done, he insisted that the cellar he had lived in for almost a year be barricaded.

For the next year, he built around it until its walls were strong, sturdy, and tough enough. People thought he had overcome his passion for the peasant girl and was growing into a man worthy of his name and heritage. When the fortress was complete, the young lord was visited by the peasant girl's husband on an urgent inquiry—his wife was missing, and they wanted to search the house. The young lord's eyes flashed with temper, but he invited them to go ahead. Disappointed in not being able to find his wife, the man went away. As the staff lessened over the years, only a butler was left, and he was instructed not to let anyone in.

Years later, when the butler died and his keys were discovered, a secret underground passageway connecting the castle's cellar to the forest was found. Inside this passage was a large room full of books and instruments, a woman's wardrobe with beautiful clothes and accessories, and some maps on a desk. But on the bed lay a man's and a woman's skeleton, holding each other even as their bones were crumbling. No one knew what to make of this except a theory—"what if a happily ever after did actually happen?"

Inspired by Château d'Ussé, France

Der Rost der Skelette

Es war einmal, in einer Zeit, die noch nicht aufgezeichnet wurde, ein Herrscher, der eine Holzfestung baute und dort bis zu seinem Tod lebte. Er ging als grausam, böse und ungewöhnlich intelligent in Erinnerung, sodass sogar seine Feinde ihn fürchteten. In seiner Jugend war er jedoch anders gewesen—bis er sich verliebte. Sie war eine Bäuerin, die bei den Festen seiner Familie sang. Als seine Mutter bemerkte, dass er sich in eine Bürgerliche verliebt hatte, arrangierte sie schnell eine heimliche Hochzeit für das Mädchen.

Aber das Mädchen liebte den jungen Lord und teilte ihm die Entscheidung mit, indem sie eine Nachricht an der Rinde des Baumes hinterließ, unter dem sie sich oft trafen, um ungestört zu sprechen. Wütend sagte er ihr, sie solle zu Beginn der Mondstunde auf ihn warten. Dann konfrontierte er seine Mutter in einem Anfall seiner berühmten Wut.

Aus Angst, ihr Sohn könnte etwas tun, was sie nicht gutheißen würde, ließ sie ihn in einen Weinkeller sperren. Tagelang schrie und heulte er und schlug gegen die Tür. Als die Bediensteten die Mutter anflehten, ihn freizulassen, lehnte sie ab und sagte, sie würde es in ein paar Monaten tun. Im Herrenhaus verbreitete sich das Gerücht, der junge Lord habe den Verstand verloren—und das hatte er auch. Mit bloßen Händen begann er, sich einen Weg aus dem Keller zu graben. Das Mädchen wurde unterdessen gegen ihren Willen verheiratet.

Da sie glaubte, ihre Liebe habe sie verlassen, stellte sie alle Uhren in ihrem neuen Zuhause auf den Zeitpunkt, an dem sie und er sich verabredet hatten. Wenn jemand versuchte, sie vorwärts zu stellen, wurde sie hysterisch, sodass alle sie so ließen, wie sie waren, und ihre Armbanduhren vor ihr versteckten. Ihr neuer Ehemann liebte sie nicht und sah keinen Sinn darin, herauszufinden, was mit ihr los war.

Er ließ sie allein, damit sie alleine im Wald umherirren konnte, da er glaubte, sie sei psychisch labil.

Dann, eines Tages, starb die Mutter des jungen Lords in einer besonders stürmischen Nacht. Als die Bediensteten den Keller öffneten, um ihren Herrn zu informieren, fanden sie einen ruhigen und gefassten jungen Mann vor sich sitzen. Er weigerte sich, den Leichnam seiner Mutter zu sehen, und wollte, dass die Beerdigung schnell über die Bühne ging.

Das war nicht überraschend, da jeder wusste, was seine Mutter getan hatte. Nachdem dies erledigt war, bestand er darauf, dass der Keller, in dem er fast ein Jahr lang gelebt hatte, verbarrikadiert wurde. Im Laufe des nächsten Jahres baute er um ihn herum, bis die Mauern stark, stabil und robust genug waren. Die Leute dachten, er habe seine Leidenschaft für das Bauernmädchen überwunden und würde zu einem Mann heranwachsen, der seines Namens und seines Erbes würdig war.

Als die Festung fertiggestellt war, erhielt der junge Herr Besuch vom Ehemann des Bauernmädchens, der eine dringende Anfrage hatte: Seine Frau war verschwunden, und sie wollten das Haus durchsuchen. Die Augen des jungen Lords blitzten vor Wut, aber er lud sie ein, fortzufahren. Enttäuscht, seine Frau nicht finden zu können, ging der Mann weg. Im Laufe der Jahre wurde das Personal immer weniger, bis nur noch ein Butler übrig war, der angewiesen wurde, niemanden hereinzulassen.

Jahre später, als der Butler starb und seine Schlüssel gefunden wurden, entdeckte man einen geheimen unterirdischen Gang, der den Keller des Schlosses mit dem Wald verband.

∞

In diesem Gang befand sich ein großer Raum voller Bücher und Instrumente, eine Damengarderobe mit schönen Kleidern und Accessoires sowie einige Karten auf einem Schreibtisch. Auf dem Bett lagen jedoch die Skelette eines Mannes und einer

Frau, die sich selbst dann noch umarmten, als ihre Knochen bereits zerfallen waren. Niemand wusste, was man davon halten sollte, außer einer Theorie: „Was wäre, wenn es tatsächlich ein Happy End gegeben hätte?"

Inspiriert vom Château d'Ussé, Frankreich

Rugina Scheletelor

Odată, într-o vreme încă neînregistrată, un lord a construit o fortăreaţă din lemn, unde a rămas până la moarte. Era cunoscut ca fiind crud, rău şi neobişnuit de inteligent, încât chiar şi duşmanii lui se temeau de el.

În tinereţe, însă, era altfel, până când s-a îndrăgostit. Ea era o ţărancă care cânta la petrecerile familiei lui. Când mama lui a realizat că se îndrăgostise de o femeie de rând, a aranjat repede ca fata să se căsătorească în secret. Dar fata era îndrăgostită de tânărul lord şi i-a spus ce se hotărâse, lăsându-i un bilet pe scoarţa copacului la care se duceau adesea pentru a vorbi fără să fie auziţi. Furios, el i-a spus să-l aştepte la răsăritul lunii. Apoi s-a dus să-şi confrunte mama într-un acces de furie, pentru care era renumit.

Temându-se că fiul ei va face ceva ce ea nu aproba, l-a închis într-o pivniţă de vinuri. Timp de zile întregi, el a ţipat, a urlat şi a bătut în uşă. Când personalul a implorat-o pe mamă să-l elibereze, ea a refuzat şi a spus că o va face în câteva luni. În conac s-au răspândit zvonuri că tânărul lord îşi pierduse minţile—şi aşa era. Cu mâinile goale, a început să sape o ieşire din pivniţă.

Între timp, fata a fost măritată împotriva voinţei ei. Crezând că iubitul ei o părăsise, a oprit toate ceasurile din noua ei casă la ora la care el şi ea stabiliseră să se întâlnească. Când cineva încerca să le pună în funcţiune, ea devenea isterică, aşa că toţi le lăsau aşa cum erau şi îşi ascundeau ceasurile de mână în jurul ei. Noul ei soţ nu era îndrăgostit de ea şi nu vedea rostul să încerce să afle ce se întâmplase. O lăsa singură să rătăcească prin pădure, crezând că era instabilă psihic.

Apoi, într-o zi, mama tânărului lord a murit într-o noapte deosebit de furtunoasă. Când personalul a deschis pivniţa pentru a-l informa pe lord, l-au găsit pe tânărul calm şi stăpân pe sine, aşezat în faţa lor. El a refuzat să vadă trupul mamei sale şi a dorit ca înmormântarea să se termine cât mai repede. Acest lucru nu era neaşteptat, având în vedere că toată lumea ştia ce făcuse mama lui. Odată ce acest lucru s-a întâmplat, el a insistat ca pivniţa în care locuise aproape un an să fie baricadată.

În anul următor, a construit în jurul ei până când zidurile au devenit puternice, solide şi suficient de rezistente. Oamenii credeau că îşi depăşise pasiunea pentru fata de la ţară şi că devenea un bărbat demn de numele şi moştenirea sa. Când fortăreaţa a fost terminată, tânărul lord a primit vizita soţului fetei de la ţară, care avea o cerere urgentă: soţia lui dispăruse şi voiau să caute în casă. Ochii tânărului lord au strălucit de furie, dar i-a invitat să intre. Dezamăgit că nu şi-a găsit soţia, bărbatul a plecat. Pe măsură ce personalul s-a redus de-a lungul anilor, a rămas doar un majordom, căruia i s-a dat instrucţiuni să nu lase pe nimeni să intre. Ani mai târziu, când majordomul a murit şi cheile lui au fost descoperite, s-a găsit un pasaj secret subteran care lega pivniţa castelului de pădure.

În interiorul acestui pasaj se afla o cameră mare plină de cărţi şi instrumente, un dulap de damă cu haine şi accesorii frumoase şi câteva hărţi pe un birou. Dar pe pat zăceau scheletele unui bărbat şi ale unei femei, îmbrăţişându-se chiar şi atunci când oasele lor se sfărâmau. Nimeni nu ştia ce să creadă despre asta, cu excepţia unei teorii: „Ce-ar fi dacă ar fi existat într-adevăr un final fericit?"

Inspirat de Château d'Ussé, Franţa

A Mermaid's Fire

Once upon a time, a boy found a beautiful mermaid washed up on the shore. Surprised and a bit scared, he started to back away instinctively until he realized that she was hurt.

Bravely, he approached her even when she drew an ivory knife. Gently, he told her he only intended to clean her wounds. When she nodded in permission, he carefully applied some medicine to her deep cuts and bandaged them with strips from his own shirt. Ever since then, they became friends. He protected the knowledge of her presence, and she would bring him pearls and precious stones to sell. He grew rich and forgot about the friend who had helped him. But the mermaid did not. She came every day to the same spot, hoping he would arrive.

One day, some fishermen in the village saw her and laid a trap to catch her. When they did, they cruelly dragged her through the streets as though she were a toy. Frightened and crying, she suddenly caught sight of her childhood friend. Stretching her hands to him, she looked at him with hopeful eyes, but he acted as if he hadn't seen her. More heartbroken by that betrayal, the mermaid cursed every single person who stayed in the village.

As she began to suffocate without the sea close by, fire began to burn through her, causing the people to run and save what they could. But not a single one who had watched her humiliation survived the fire.

Inspired by Conwy Castle, United Kingdom

Das Feuer einer Meerjungfrau

Es war einmal ein Junge, der eine wunderschöne Meerjungfrau fand, die an den Strand gespült worden war. Überrascht und ein wenig verängstigt wich er instinktiv zurück, bis er bemerkte, dass sie verletzt war.

Tapfer näherte er sich ihr, obwohl sie ein Elfenbeinmesser zog. Sanft erklärte er ihr, dass er nur ihre Wunden reinigen wolle. Als sie zustimmend nickte, trug er vorsichtig etwas Medizin auf ihre tiefen Schnitte auf und verband sie mit Streifen seines eigenen Hemdes. Seitdem wurden sie Freunde. Er bewahrte das Wissen um ihre Existenz, und sie brachte ihm Perlen und Edelsteine, die er verkaufen konnte. Er wurde reich und vergaß die Freundin, die ihm geholfen hatte. Aber die Meerjungfrau vergaß ihn nicht. Sie kam jeden Tag an denselben Ort, in der Hoffnung, dass er kommen würde.

Eines Tages sahen einige Fischer aus dem Dorf sie und stellten ihr eine Falle, um sie zu fangen. Als sie das geschafft hatten, zerrten sie sie grausam durch die Straßen, als wäre sie ein Spielzeug. Verängstigt und weinend erblickte sie plötzlich ihren Freund aus Kindertagen. Sie streckte ihre Hände nach ihm aus und sah ihn mit hoffnungsvollen Augen an, aber er tat so, als hätte er sie nicht gesehen. Noch mehr gebrochenen Herzens durch diesen Verrat verfluchte die Meerjungfrau jeden einzelnen Menschen, der im Dorf geblieben war.

Als sie ohne das Meer in ihrer Nähe zu ersticken begann, begann ein Feuer in ihr zu brennen, das die Menschen dazu veranlasste, zu fliehen und zu retten, was sie konnten. Aber keiner, der ihre Demütigung mit angesehen hatte, überlebte das Feuer.

Inspiriert von Conwy Castle, Vereinigtes Königreich

Focul unei Sirene

A fost odată ca niciodată, un băiat care a găsit o frumoasă sirenă eşuată pe ţărm. Surprins şi puţin speriat, a început să se retragă instinctiv, până când şi-a dat seama că ea era rănită.

Cu curaj, s-a apropiat de ea, chiar şi atunci când ea a scos un cuţit de fildeş. Cu blândeţe, i-a spus că intenţiona doar să-i cureţe rănile. Când ea a dat din cap în semn de aprobare, el i-a aplicat cu grijă nişte medicamente pe tăieturile adânci şi le-a bandajat cu fâşii din propria cămaşă. De atunci, au devenit prieteni. El a păstrat secretul prezenţei ei, iar ea îi aducea perle şi pietre preţioase pe care el le vindea. El s-a îmbogăţit şi a uitat de prietena care îl ajutase. Dar sirena nu a uitat. Ea venea în fiecare zi în acelaşi loc, sperând că el va veni.

Într-o zi, nişte pescari din sat au văzut-o şi i-au întins o capcană pentru a o prinde. Când au reuşit, au târât-o cu cruzime pe străzi, ca şi cum ar fi fost o jucărie. Speriată şi plângând, ea l-a zărit brusc pe prietenul ei din copilărie. Întinzându-şi mâinile spre el, l-a privit cu ochi plini de speranţă, dar el s-a comportat de parcă nu o văzuse. Cu inima frântă de această trădare, sirena i-a blestemat pe toţi cei care locuiau în sat.

Pe măsură ce începea să se sufoce fără marea aproape, focul a început să o mistuie, determinându-i pe oameni să fugă şi să salveze ce puteau. Dar niciunul dintre cei care au asistat la umilirea ei nu a supravieţuit incendiului.

Inspirat de Castelul Conwy, Regatul Unit

Gentle Ghost

Once upon a time, there was a lady who lived in a castle with just a few members of staff on hand to take care of her and the grounds.

She herself was known to wear only silver. She refused to wear any other colour. Her chambermaid thought it was because her hair was naturally silver-white, and because all the lady's dresses and shoes in the cupboard were silver. She rarely gave instructions to tend to her and preferred to do everything herself, including getting food from the kitchen pantry. This peculiar behaviour made the staff think she was eccentric, but they did not complain, as she rarely bothered them for anything. She was never seen in the day, but when she appeared in the evenings, she spoke to everyone with compassion and thoughtfulness. No one had a bad thing to say about her—except they wondered about the sound of her cries in the night.

It was only the arrival of the current lady of the house that filled their hearts with dread—when she told them the person they were talking about was dead.

Inspired by Conwy Castle, United Kingdom

Der Sanfte Geist

Es war einmal eine Dame, die in einem Schloss lebte, wo nur wenige Bedienstete für sie und das Anwesen sorgten.

Sie selbst trug bekanntermaßen ausschließlich Silber. Sie weigerte sich, andere Farben zu tragen. Ihre Kammerzofe vermutete, dass dies daran lag, dass ihr Haar von Natur aus silberweiß war und alle Kleider und Schuhe der Dame im Schrank silbern waren. Sie gab selten Anweisungen, sich um sie zu kümmern, und zog es vor, alles selbst zu tun, einschließlich der Beschaffung von Lebensmitteln aus der Küchenvorratskammer. Dieses seltsame Verhalten ließ die Bediensteten denken, sie sei exzentrisch, aber sie beschwerten sich nicht, da sie sie selten mit irgendetwas belästigte. Tagsüber war sie nie zu sehen, aber wenn sie abends erschien, sprach sie mit allen mit Mitgefühl und Nachdenklichkeit. Niemand hatte etwas Schlechtes über sie zu sagen—außer dass sie sich über das Geräusch ihrer Schreie in der Nacht wunderten.

Erst die Ankunft der derzeitigen Hausherrin erfüllte ihre Herzen mit Schrecken—als sie ihnen erzählte, dass die Person, über die sie sprachen, tot sei.

Inspiriert von Conwy Castle, Vereinigtes Königreich

Fantoma Blândă

A fost odată ca niciodată o doamnă care locuia într-un castel, având la dispoziţie doar câţiva angajaţi care aveau grijă de ea şi de proprietate.

Era cunoscută pentru faptul că purta numai argintiu. Refuza să poarte orice altă culoare. Camerista ei credea că motivul era faptul că părul ei era natural argintiu-alb, iar toate rochiile şi pantofii doamnei din dulap erau argintii. Rar dădea instrucţiuni pentru îngrijirea ei şi prefera să facă totul singură, inclusiv să-şi ia mâncarea din cămara bucătăriei. Acest comportament ciudat îi făcea pe angajaţi să creadă că era excentrică, dar nu se plângeau, deoarece rareori îi deranja cu ceva. Nu era văzută niciodată în timpul zilei, dar când apărea seara, vorbea cu toată lumea cu compasiune şi atenţie. Nimeni nu avea nimic rău de spus despre ea, cu excepţia faptului că se întrebau ce era cu sunetul plânsetelor ei din timpul nopţii.

Doar sosirea actualei stăpâne a casei le-a umplut inimile de teamă—când le-a spus că persoana despre care vorbeau era moartă.

Inspirat de Castelul Conwy, Regatul Unit

A Knight's Justice

Once upon a time, there was a soldier who loved a princess. She was betrothed to marry a future king. To love royalty was like asking if it were possible to marry the sun.

The princess was no ordinary woman—she was fierce, strong, and wild. The soldier himself had once been a rebel, but he had become docile, passive, and obedient to the king because he wanted to stay close to her.

The soldier grew in rank patiently, and when he became a knight, he was given the honour of protecting the princess. Until the day she broke convention. She refused his protection and asked instead for him to be hers. He refused out of honour—not because he did not want to say yes.

A spy in the army noted this conversation and whispered it into the king's ear. Without hearing the accused, the king ordered the knight's execution for the following morning.

Horrified, the princess went to visit the prison that very evening. After persuading the guards to allow her to see the knight for a moment, she made him exchange clothes with her and promised him that she would be safe from her father's wrath.

But she miscalculated the nature of her father's wickedness. To make sure the knight did not die with any honour or be witnessed by the public, he ordered poison to be placed in the knight's jar of water and food. Unknowingly, the princess drank the water and died instantly by her own father's hand.

When the knight heard of the manner of her death, his rage knew no bounds.

He incited the whole kingdom to attack the castle, and a massive slaughter followed—for the princess was loved not only by the people outside her walls but within.

Almost dying from the wounds he had sustained to his back and chest while fighting to reach the craven king—who was hiding in a soldier's armour—the knight drew his sword. With a single swipe, he severed the king's head before dying a few minutes later.

And though the legend tells of a headless soldier walking the castle's dimly lit corridors, it is actually the cowardly king still trying to escape the justice already dealt to him.

Inspired by Conwy Castle, United Kingdom

Die Gerechtigkeit eines Ritters

Es war einmal ein Soldat, der eine Prinzessin liebte. Sie war mit einem zukünftigen König verlobt. Einen König zu lieben war wie zu fragen, ob es möglich wäre, die Sonne zu heiraten.

Die Prinzessin war keine gewöhnliche Frau—sie war wild, stark und ungestüm. Der Soldat selbst war einst ein Rebell gewesen, aber er war fügsam, passiv und dem König gehorsam geworden, weil er in ihrer Nähe bleiben wollte.

Der Soldat stieg geduldig in den Rängen auf, und als er zum Ritter geschlagen wurde, erhielt er die Ehre, die Prinzessin zu beschützen. Bis zu dem Tag, an dem sie mit den Konventionen brach. Sie lehnte seinen Schutz ab und bat ihn stattdessen, ihr zu gehören. Er lehnte aus Ehrgefühl ab—nicht, weil er nicht Ja sagen wollte.

Ein Spion in der Armee bemerkte dieses Gespräch und flüsterte es dem König ins Ohr. Ohne den Angeklagten anzuhören, ordnete der König die Hinrichtung des Ritters für den nächsten Morgen an.

Entsetzt besuchte die Prinzessin noch am selben Abend das Gefängnis. Nachdem sie die Wachen überredet hatte, sie den Ritter für einen Moment sehen zu lassen, ließ sie ihn mit ihr die Kleidung tauschen und versprach ihm, dass sie vor dem Zorn ihres Vaters sicher sein würde.

Doch sie hatte die Boshaftigkeit ihres Vaters falsch eingeschätzt. Um sicherzustellen, dass der Ritter nicht in Ehren starb und nicht von der Öffentlichkeit gesehen wurde, befahl er, Gift in den Wasserkrug und das Essen des Ritters zu geben. Ohne es zu wissen, trank die Prinzessin das Wasser und starb augenblicklich durch die Hand ihres eigenen Vaters.

∞

Als der Ritter von der Art ihres Todes erfuhr, kannte seine Wut keine Grenzen mehr. Er stachelte das ganze Königreich dazu an, die Burg anzugreifen, und es kam zu einem massiven Gemetzel—denn die Prinzessin wurde nicht nur von den Menschen außerhalb der Burgmauern geliebt, sondern auch von denen innerhalb.

Der Ritter, der fast an den Wunden starb, die er sich beim Kampf um den feigen König, der sich in einer Soldatenrüstung versteckt hatte, an Rücken und Brust zugezogen hatte, zog sein Schwert. Mit einem einzigen Hieb schlug er dem König den Kopf ab, bevor er wenige Minuten später starb.

Und obwohl die Legende von einem kopflosen Soldaten erzählt, der durch die schummrigen Korridore der Burg wandelt, handelt es sich in Wirklichkeit um den feigen König, der immer noch versucht, der Gerechtigkeit zu entkommen, die ihm bereits widerfahren ist.

Inspiriert von Conwy Castle, Vereinigtes Königreich

Dreptatea unui Cavaler

A fost odată ca niciodată un soldat care iubea o prinţesă. Ea era logodită cu viitorul rege. A iubi un membru al familiei regale era ca şi cum ai întreba dacă este posibil să te căsătoreşti cu soarele.

Prinţesa nu era o femeie obişnuită—era aprigă, puternică şi sălbatică. Soldatul fusese odată un rebel, dar devenise docil, pasiv şi ascultător faţă de rege, pentru că voia să rămână aproape de ea.

Soldatul a avansat cu răbdare în grad şi, când a devenit cavaler, i s-a acordat onoarea de a o proteja pe prinţesă. Până în ziua în care ea a încălcat convenţiile. Ea a refuzat protecţia lui şi i-a cerut în schimb să fie al ei. El a refuzat din motive de onoare, nu pentru că nu voia să accepte.

Un spion din armată a observat această conversaţie şi i-a şoptit-o regelui la ureche. Fără să-l asculte pe acuzat, regele a ordonat execuţia cavalerului pentru dimineaţa următoare.

Îngrozită, prinţesa s-a dus să viziteze închisoarea în aceeaşi seară. După ce i-a convins pe gardieni să o lase să-l vadă pe cavaler pentru o clipă, l-a convins să facă schimb de haine cu ea şi i-a promis că va fi în siguranţă faţă de mânia tatălui ei.

Dar ea a calculat greşit natura răutăţii tatălui său. Pentru a se asigura că cavalerul nu va muri cu onoare şi nu va fi văzut de public, el a ordonat să se pună otravă în vasul cu apă şi mâncare al cavalerului. Fără să ştie, prinţesa a băut apa şi a murit instantaneu din mâna propriului tată.

Când cavalerul a auzit de modul în care a murit ea, furia lui nu a mai cunoscut limite.

El a incitat întregul regat să atace castelul, iar apoi a urmat un masacru în masă, deoarece prinţesa era iubită nu numai de oamenii din afara zidurilor, ci şi de cei din interior.

Aproape murind din cauza rănilor pe care le suferise la spate şi la piept în timp ce lupta să ajungă la regele laş, care se ascundea într-o armură de soldat, cavalerul şi-a scos sabia. Cu o singură lovitură, i-a tăiat capul regelui înainte de a muri câteva minute mai târziu.

Şi deşi legenda povesteşte despre un soldat fără cap care umblă pe coridoarele slab iluminate ale castelului, acesta este de fapt regele laş care încă încearcă să scape de pedeapsa care i-a fost deja aplicată.

Inspirat de Castelul Conwy, Regatul Unit

Foolish Monk

Once upon a time, in a castle far away, lived a monk. This monk was unlike any other, for he had a secret he was unwilling to share. He was in lovebut because he was a monk, he knew it was forbidden. Instead of sharing his troubles or crisis with a superior, or meeting it with honesty, he chose to ignore it.

But the more he tried to resist, the more obsessed he became with avoiding it. The very fact that he could not accept the parts of himself that also held who he was not ultimately made it hard for him to fight against what he believed he was already doing, when in reality, he was confusing denial of his feelings for integrity.

As his struggles continued, his choices grew darker. He tried to hide who he was in love with but ended up exposing that he was not immune to love. Distraught, he flung himself over the west tower's edge, convinced that he was not worthy to be a monk.

As the rest of his brothers stood by his coffin, sadness held their heartsand they wished he had confided in them, for they knew they could have shown him that to overcome the feelings he couldn't accept was through the simple act of accepting that they were there.

Inspired by Conwy Castle, United Kingdom

∞

Der Törichte Mönch

Es war einmal ein Mönch, der in einem weit entfernten Schloss lebte. Dieser Mönch war anders als alle anderen, denn er hatte ein Geheimnis, das er nicht preisgeben wollte. Er war verliebt, aber da er Mönch war, wusste er, dass dies verboten war. Anstatt seine Probleme und seine Krise mit einem Vorgesetzten zu besprechen oder sich ehrlich damit auseinanderzusetzen, entschied er sich, sie zu ignorieren.

Doch je mehr er versuchte, sich zu wehren, desto mehr wurde er davon besessen, sie zu vermeiden. Die Tatsache, dass er die Teile seiner selbst, die nicht zu ihm passten, nicht akzeptieren konnte, machte es ihm letztendlich schwer, gegen das anzukämpfen, was er seiner Meinung nach bereits tat, obwohl er in Wirklichkeit die Verleugnung seiner Gefühle mit Integrität verwechselte.

Je länger sein Kampf andauerte, desto düsterer wurden seine Entscheidungen. Er versuchte zu verbergen, wen er liebte, entlarvte sich damit aber nur selbst als nicht immun gegen die Liebe. Verzweifelt stürzte er sich über den Rand des Westturms, überzeugt davon, dass er es nicht wert war, Mönch zu sein.

Als seine Mitbrüder um seinen Sarg standen, erfüllte Traurigkeit ihre Herzen und sie wünschten sich, er hätte sich ihnen anvertraut, denn sie wussten, dass sie ihm hätten zeigen können, dass er seine Gefühle, die er nicht akzeptieren konnte, überwinden konnte, indem er einfach akzeptierte, dass sie da waren.

Inspiriert von Conwy Castle, Vereinigtes Königreich

Călugărul Nebun

A fost odată, într-un castel îndepărtat, un călugăr. Acest călugăr era diferit de ceilalţi, pentru că avea un secret pe care nu voia să-l împărtăşească. Era îndrăgostit, dar, fiind călugăr, ştia că era interzis. În loc să-şi împărtăşească problemele sau criza cu un superior sau să le înfrunte cu sinceritate, a ales să le ignore.

Cu cât încerca mai mult să reziste, cu atât devenea mai obsedat de a le evita. Faptul că nu putea accepta părţile din el care nu îl reprezentau îl făcea să lupte împotriva a ceea ce credea că deja făcea, când, în realitate, confunda negarea sentimentelor sale cu integritatea.

Pe măsură ce lupta lui continua, alegerile lui deveneau din ce în ce mai întunecate. A încercat să ascundă persoana pe care o iubea, dar a sfârşit prin a dezvălui că nu era imun la dragoste. Într-o stare de disperare, s-a aruncat de pe marginea turnului de vest, convins că nu era demn să fie călugăr.

În timp ce ceilalţi fraţi stăteau lângă sicriul său, tristeţea le cuprinse inimile şi îşi doreau ca el să le fi mărturisit, pentru că ştiau că i-ar fi putut arăta că pentru a depăşi sentimentele pe care nu le putea accepta era suficient să le accepte pur şi simplu.

Inspirat de Castelul Conwy, Regatul Unit

White Governess

Once upon a time, there were two royal children who fell to their deaths from one of the towers that was being repaired.

Their governess was said to have pushed them to secure the throne for another childunder whose instructions, no one knows. Others said she had tried to stop them when they were playing a dangerous game in the forbidden tower. Their deaths found her guilty, for whether or not she caused them, she was responsible, as they had been in her care.

After she was hung in the same tower by order of the King, she and the children were described as white figures appearing in the tower from where they all met their fateful end.

The staff were known to say that the fact that they appear together suggests her innocence. It is said that they only show themselves when treachery or ill intentions lurk within the castle walls.

Inspired by Conwy Castle, United Kingdom

Die Weiße Gouvernante

Es waren einmal zwei königliche Kinder, die von einem der Türme, der gerade renoviert wurde, in den Tod stürzten.

Ihre Gouvernante soll sie gestoßen haben, um den Thron für ein anderes Kind zu sichern, auf wessen Anweisung hin, weiß niemand. Andere sagten, sie habe versucht, sie aufzuhalten, als sie in dem verbotenen Turm ein gefährliches Spiel spielten. Ihr Tod machte sie schuldig, denn unabhängig davon, ob sie ihn verursacht hatte oder nicht, war sie verantwortlich, da sie für sie verantwortlich war.

Nachdem sie auf Befehl des Königs in demselben Turm gehängt worden war, wurden sie und die Kinder als weiße Gestalten beschrieben, die in dem Turm erschienen, in dem sie alle ihr schicksalhaftes Ende gefunden hatten.

Die Bediensteten sagten, dass die Tatsache, dass sie zusammen erscheinen, auf ihre Unschuld hindeute. Es heißt, dass sie sich nur zeigen, wenn Verrat oder böse Absichten innerhalb der Burgmauern lauern.

Inspiriert von Conwy Castle, Vereinigtes Königreich

Guvernanta Albă

A fost odată ca niciodată, doi copii regali care au căzut în gol de pe unul dintre turnurile care erau în reparaţie.

Se spune că guvernanta lor i-ar fi împins pentru a asigura tronul unui alt copil, la ordinul cui, nimeni nu ştie. Alţii spun că ea a încercat să-i oprească când se jucau un joc periculos în turnul interzis. Moartea lor a făcut-o vinovată, pentru că, indiferent dacă ea a provocat-o sau nu, era responsabilă, deoarece copiii erau în grija ei.

După ce a fost spânzurată în acelaşi turn din ordinul regelui, ea şi copiii au fost descrişi ca fiind siluete albe care apăreau în turnul în care şi-au găsit sfârşitul tragic.

Personalul spunea că faptul că apar împreună sugerează nevinovăţia ei. Se spune că ei se arată doar când în interiorul zidurilor castelului se ascund trădarea sau intenţii rele.

Inspirat de Castelul Conwy, Regatul Unit

Count Rakulace

Once upon a time, there was a mysterious castle in India that had been built by a clever scientist. He filled it with rooms of wonder, intrigue, and dread, for he liked people to marvel at inventions and ideasor at least, to become curious.

One of his inventions was a secret tunnel engineered to carry water up into the castle, while another was called the revolving room, which would rotate depending on the force of the wind. There was also a clock whose hands would point toward people who were feeling heavy.

The scientist was given the name Count Rakulace because of his love for creativity, his enjoyment of comfort, and his quick wit. His work was either never recorded or perhaps stolen or lostfor no one knows what truly happened to him.

As the years passed, the castle took on the appearance of being abandoned. Travellers who passed by said the air around it felt almost gothic.

Inspired by Chiktan Castle, India

Graf Rakulace

Es war einmal ein geheimnisvolles Schloss in Indien, das von einem klugen Wissenschaftler erbaut worden war. Er füllte es mit Räumen voller Wunder, Intrigen und Schrecken, denn er mochte es, wenn Menschen seine Erfindungen und Ideen bestaunten—oder zumindest neugierig wurden.

Eine seiner Erfindungen war ein geheimer Tunnel, der Wasser in das Schloss beförderte, eine andere war der sogenannte Drehraum, der sich je nach Windstärke drehte. Es gab auch eine Uhr, deren Zeiger auf Menschen zeigte, die sich schwer fühlten.

Der Wissenschaftler erhielt den Namen Graf Rakulace aufgrund seiner Liebe zur Kreativität, seiner Vorliebe für Komfort und seines schnellen Verstands. Seine Arbeit wurde entweder nie aufgezeichnet oder vielleicht gestohlen oder ging verloren, denn niemand weiß, was wirklich mit ihm geschehen ist.

Im Laufe der Jahre sah das Schloss zunehmend verlassen aus. Reisende, die daran vorbeikamen, sagten, die Atmosphäre um das Schloss herum sei fast gotisch.

Inspiriert von Chiktan Castle, Indien

Contele Rakulace

A fost odată ca niciodată un castel misterios în India, construit de un savant inteligent. El l-a umplut cu camere pline de minuni, intrigi şi teamă, pentru că îi plăcea ca oamenii să se minuneze de invenţii şi idei sau, cel puţin, să devină curioşi.

Una dintre invenţiile sale era un tunel secret conceput pentru a transporta apa în castel, iar alta era numită camera rotativă, care se rotea în funcţie de forţa vântului. Mai era şi un ceas ale cărui limbi arătau spre persoanele care se simţeau grele.

Omului de ştiinţă i s-a dat numele de contele Rakulace datorită dragostei sale pentru creativitate, plăcerii sale pentru confort şi inteligenţei sale rapide. Munca sa nu a fost niciodată înregistrată sau poate a fost furată sau pierdută, pentru că nimeni nu ştie ce s-a întâmplat cu adevărat cu el.

Odată cu trecerea anilor, castelul a căpătat aspectul unui loc abandonat. Călătorii care treceau pe lângă el spuneau că atmosfera din jurul său era aproape gotică.

Inspirat de Castelul Chiktan, India

Brave Warrior

Once upon a time, artists were inspired by a King's bravery during a warbut maybe there is another story behind why.

The young heir had always given up when things were tough. He had grown up with everyone catering to him until he met a wise man who told him he shouldn't act so spoiled, for no king was more superior than his subjects. "If your people are willing to die for you," the wise man said, "shouldn't you be the first to be willing to die for them?"

The young King thought deeply about this. Instead of becoming angry, he asked what he should do to become a ruler worthy of his people. The wise man smiled and replied, "Leadbut be willing to do what those in your service are willing to do as well."

The King was a quick learner, and over time, he earned the love and respect of his soldiers. One day in battle, an explosion on the flagship left him severely wounded in thirteen places. He lost his right eye, yet he did not retreat to safety despite his youth. Instead, he stood with his army and cheered them on to victory.

This act of resilience was remembered in murals and retold everywhere, for a King's courageous presence in battle is more powerful than any ordinary soldier facing the sword.

Inspired by Frederiksborg Castle, Denmark

Der Tapfere Krieger

Es war einmal ein König, dessen Tapferkeit während eines Krieges Künstler inspirierte—aber vielleicht steckt noch eine andere Geschichte dahinter.

Der junge Thronfolger hatte immer aufgegeben, wenn es schwierig wurde. Er war damit aufgewachsen, dass sich alle um ihn kümmerten, bis er einen weisen Mann traf, der ihm sagte, er solle sich nicht so verwöhnt benehmen, denn kein König sei seinen Untertanen überlegen. „Wenn dein Volk bereit ist, für dich zu sterben", sagte der Weise, „solltest du dann nicht der Erste sein, der bereit ist, für sie zu sterben?"

Der junge König dachte tief darüber nach. Anstatt wütend zu werden, fragte er, was er tun müsse, um ein Herrscher zu werden, der seines Volkes würdig sei. Der Weise lächelte und antwortete: „Führe, aber sei bereit, das zu tun, was auch diejenigen tun, die dir dienen."

Der König lernte schnell und gewann mit der Zeit die Liebe und den Respekt seiner Soldaten. Eines Tages wurde er in einer Schlacht durch eine Explosion auf dem Flaggschiff an dreizehn Stellen schwer verletzt. Er verlor sein rechtes Auge, zog sich aber trotz seiner Jugend nicht in Sicherheit zurück. Stattdessen stand er mit seiner Armee auf dem Schlachtfeld und feuerte sie zum Sieg an.

Diese Tat der Widerstandsfähigkeit wurde in Wandgemälden verewigt und überall weitererzählt, denn die mutige Präsenz eines Königs in der Schlacht ist mächtiger als die eines gewöhnlichen Soldaten, der sich dem Schwert stellt.

Inspiriert vom Schloss Frederiksborg, Dänemark

Războinicul Curajos

Odată ca niciodată, artiştii au fost inspiraţi de curajul unui rege în timpul unui război, dar poate că există o altă poveste în spatele acestui motiv.

Tânărul moştenitor renunţa întotdeauna când lucrurile deveneau dificile. Crescuse cu toată lumea care îl răsfăţa, până când a întâlnit un înţelept care i-a spus că nu ar trebui să se comporte atât de răsfăţat, pentru că niciun rege nu era superior supuşilor săi. „Dacă poporul tău este dispus să moară pentru tine", a spus înţeleptul, „nu ar trebui să fii tu primul dispus să mori pentru ei?"

Tânărul rege s-a gândit profund la acest lucru. În loc să se supere, a întrebat ce ar trebui să facă pentru a deveni un conducător demn de poporul său. Înţeleptul a zâmbit și a răspuns: „Condu, dar fii dispus să faci ceea ce sunt dispuși să facă și cei care te slujesc".

Regele învăţa repede și, în timp, a câștigat dragostea și respectul soldaţilor săi. Într-o zi, în timpul unei bătălii, o explozie pe nava amiral l-a rănit grav în treisprezece locuri. Şi-a pierdut ochiul drept, dar, în ciuda tinereţii sale, nu s-a retras în siguranţă. În schimb, a rămas alături de armata sa și i-a încurajat să obţină victoria.

Acest act de rezilienţă a fost imortalizat în picturi murale și povestit peste tot, pentru că prezenţa curajoasă a unui rege în luptă este mai puternică decât orice soldat obișnuit care înfruntă sabia.

Inspirat de Castelul Frederiksborg, Danemarca

Rain Queen

Once upon a time, there lived a beautiful Queen. She was not only physically attractive but was also known to be kind, generous, and loyal to those who served her. She was known to be introverted, even when she took her public office seriously. She had been married at fifteen to a King she had never met, and since he had never visited her, five years had passed without her thinking too much about it.

One day, she received a notice that he would be arriving and that she was to move to a castle that would be hers the moment she stepped inside. This was the King's gift to her.

Anxious but ready, the young Queen looked forward to the next chapter in her life. The only things she took with her from her childhood home were two gray kittens that had been born a few weeks ago, a sentimental keepsake of dried lilies she placed inside the pages of a book, and a necklace with a wing pendant that she called "her freedom."

When she met her husband, they were both surprised by how deeply they fell in love from the moment they laid eyes on each other, as this was an unusual occurrence for their generation. Though their marriage produced no children, they enjoyed spending a lot of time tending to their people and loving each other. A year later, she succumbed to pneumonia, for she would often sit for hours in the rain, refusing cover or the castle's shelter, as though waiting to join him.

It is said that till today, her ghost remains because she did not wish to leave the home where she had spent years with the man she loved, nor could she reconcile with his death.

∞

Csstle Secrets For You

Those who see her have reported her tragic beauty and peaceful spirit, and those who have only felt her presence have said that she leaves the scent of petrichor in rooms even when one cannot see her.

Inspired by Bran Castle, Romania

Reena Doss

Die Regenkönigin

Es war einmal eine wunderschöne Königin. Sie war nicht nur körperlich attraktiv, sondern auch bekannt dafür, dass sie freundlich, großzügig und loyal gegenüber denen war, die ihr dienten. Sie galt als introvertiert, auch wenn sie ihr öffentliches Amt ernst nahm. Mit fünfzehn Jahren wurde sie mit einem König verheiratet, den sie nie zuvor gesehen hatte, und da er sie nie besucht hatte, vergingen fünf Jahre, ohne dass sie sich darüber viele Gedanken machte.

Eines Tages erhielt sie die Nachricht, dass er kommen würde und dass sie in ein Schloss umziehen sollte, das ihr gehören würde, sobald sie es betreten hätte. Das war das Geschenk des Königs an sie. Die junge Königin war nervös, aber bereit und freute sich auf den nächsten Abschnitt ihres Lebens.

Das Einzige, was sie aus ihrem Elternhaus mitnahm, waren zwei graue Kätzchen, die vor einigen Wochen geboren worden waren, ein sentimentales Andenken in Form von getrockneten Lilien, das sie zwischen die Seiten eines Buches gelegt hatte, und eine Halskette mit einem Flügelanhänger, den sie „ihre Freiheit“ nannte.

Als sie ihren Ehemann kennenlernte, waren beide überrascht, wie tief sie sich vom ersten Augenblick an ineinander verliebten, da dies für ihre Generation ungewöhnlich war.

Obwohl ihre Ehe keine Kinder hervorbrachte, genossen sie es, viel Zeit damit zu verbringen, sich um ihr Volk zu kümmern und einander zu lieben. Ein Jahr später erlag sie einer Lungenentzündung, da sie oft stundenlang im Regen saß und sich weder unterstellen noch in die Burg zurückziehen wollte, als würde sie darauf warten, zu ihm zu kommen.

Es heißt, dass ihr Geist bis heute dort verweilt, weil sie das Haus, in dem sie Jahre mit dem Mann verbracht hatte, den sie liebte, nicht verlassen wollte und sich auch nicht mit seinem Tod abfinden konnte.

Diejenigen, die sie gesehen haben, berichten von ihrer tragischen Schönheit und ihrer friedlichen Ausstrahlung, und diejenigen, die nur ihre Anwesenheit gespürt haben, sagen, dass sie den Duft von Petrichor in den Räumen hinterlässt, auch wenn man sie nicht sehen kann.

Inspiriert vom Schloss Bran in Rumänien

Regina Ploii

A fost odată ca niciodată o regină frumoasă. Nu era doar frumoasă fizic, ci era cunoscută și pentru bunătatea, generozitatea și loialitatea față de cei care o slujeau. Era cunoscută ca fiind introvertită, chiar și atunci când își lua în serios funcția publică. Se căsătorise la cincisprezece ani cu un rege pe care nu-l cunoscuse niciodată, iar deoarece acesta nu o vizitase niciodată, trecuseră cinci ani fără ca ea să se gândească prea mult la asta.

Într-o zi, a primit o înștiințare că el urma să sosească și că ea trebuia să se mute într-un castel care îi va aparține din momentul în care va păși înăuntru. Acesta era cadoul regelui pentru ea.

Anxioasă, dar pregătită, tânăra regină aștepta cu nerăbdare următorul capitol din viața ei. Singurele lucruri pe care le-a luat cu ea din casa copilăriei au fost doi pisoi cenușii născuți cu câteva săptămâni în urmă, o amintire sentimentală sub forma unor crini uscați pe care i-a pus între paginile unei cărți și un colier cu un pandantiv în formă de aripă pe care îl numea „libertatea ei".

Când și-a întâlnit soțul, amândoi au fost surprinși de cât de profund s-au îndrăgostit din momentul în care s-au văzut, deoarece acest lucru era neobișnuit pentru generația lor. Deși căsătoria lor nu a dat naștere la copii, ei se bucurau să petreacă mult timp îngrijindu-și poporul și iubindu-se unul pe celălalt.

Un an mai târziu, ea a cedat în fața pneumoniei, deoarece stătea adesea ore întregi în ploaie, refuzând să se adăpostească sau să se refugieze în castel, ca și cum ar fi așteptat să se alăture lui.

∞

Se spune că până astăzi fantoma ei rămâne acolo, deoarece nu a dorit să părăsească casa în care a petrecut ani de zile alături de bărbatul pe care l-a iubit şi nici nu s-a putut împăca cu moartea lui.

Cei care o văd au povestit despre frumuseţea ei tragică şi spiritul ei paşnic, iar cei care i-au simţit doar prezenţa au spus că ea lasă mirosul de petrichor în camere, chiar şi atunci când nu o poţi vedea.

Inspirat de Castelul Bran, România

Space For You

Acknowledgements

I am grateful

Life is always better with stories. I love making up stories for children, for adults, and for those who need them the most.

When I make up a story, harder emotions can be explored, and I always add a hint—or lots—of fantasy elements. That is the power of imagination. It is what my sisters—both own and chosen—have loved the most about me, even if they are not fully aware of it.

When I was a little girl, my little sisters, cousins, and even strangers' children loved when I told a story through my art, words, or dolls. When I grew up, my friends would be highly entertained by how I could connect pathways or concepts and link them into a story on the spot. These tiny tales are just a few that I am publishing here, but there are many still unwritten. They will grow wider, longer, and deeper because that is the never-ending gift of flow in imagination. These tales were inspired by fables, myths, and legends that are already part of my heart's experiences, my mind's thoughts, and the wild spirit of adventure that leaps within me.

I want to thank my poetic friends—Miriam Otto for your words of encouragement, and Ismet Diab for your Instagram story imagery—because both of you reminded me to dream again, and to realize that this gift of writing, feeling images, and connecting them into worlds of imagination is exactly who I am meant to be in this genre.

Most importantly, I thank the Weaver for cultivating this gift, and for teaching me how powerful it becomes when I share its creations with others. How beautifully it takes root, grows, and is interpreted by others in different ways.

Reena Doss

In the beginning year (2018) of this creative journey, I did not know how to feel free of being attached to what I created until I realized that I, too, have received inspiring seeds in different forms—whether through a word of encouragement, a kind gesture, or others' creations. At first, when I saw others use what I posted, created, or published in their own style of interpretation without asking permission—or even denying that they did—I had to hold my feelings of hurt, confusion, and unnecessary anger tenderly. I knew it was an opportunity to learn the other part of creating something beautiful: that it is perfectly okay to love what we create, but this is also why letting them go is hard, because it means giving up control over how they may be used. However, it is also important to not allow yourself to be taken advantage of by others. Boundaries are necessary so that forgiveness cannot be exploited indefinitely, and a mutual way forward must be created.

In accepting that it was not up to me, I discovered that I am free to trust in the joy of seeing how a little voice like mine can make ripples. In creating with the gifts I have, I am honouring the Weaver who gave them to me. In releasing what I create, I am trusting others to use those seeds to create with the gifts that they have. And together, all of us answer to the Weaver. In obedience to the Weaver, I find a different kind of freedom in saying "I do" to His plan before any of my own.

Gratitude to my *Ink Gladiators Press' team—Leonie Belle Haw, Justin Adam Wolf* and *Aelius Arche*—for their unwavering support in using their professional skills to help me publish this book.

May the quill of hope find you in the dark,

Reena Doss

I'll find you in the dark...

Born in Calcutta with roots drawn from Chennai and Pondicherry, Reena Doss has lived most of her life in the south of India—Bangalore. Though she prefers traveling to far-off places inside her head, she sometimes ventures into the world that others call real.

Reena Doss considers writing to be her first voice of expression, followed closely by art, and creativity. Through the encouraging platform provided by the Instagram community, she reclaimed her lost voices, evolved a few others and discovered new ones along the way.

This has redeemed her trust that consistent Hope, Faith and Love in what is true ignites what is impossible to occur. Her adoration for her beloved Weaver, the Celestial Sky, Nature and her fellow Earthians has given her immeasurable courage to endure every season with a resilience born from battles overcome.

You can try and catch her but it may not always be possible as she is generally off on adventures flying on phoenix wings, swimming into the deep with mermaids and chasing fiery dragons down for stories.

To those who remain true to themselves,
to those who create magic wherever they go,
and for those who sit beside the hurt
when everyone else leaves,
Art will always immortalize you.

Please scan the QR code to follow her on Instagram @reenadossauthor
www.reenadoss.com

This little book is called a *Lantern* because love is light in disguise. It can only be found when you are buried in the dark, when the seeds die, and you choose to bravely grow and become worthy of your given name—a polished gem, a diamond that cannot help but shine. Lanterns are meant for those who need hope while they are being:

- ♥ Condemned unjustly by those who see a version they want
- ♥ Gossiped about when they are not present to defend themselves
- ♥ Taken advantage of when they were beaten down by life, by those who should have stood by them
- ♥ Judged, neglected, and persecuted while they are struggling
- ♥ Abandoned by those who willingly chose to see them as toxic because it suited their narrative
- ♥ Manipulated by those who bore false witness against them to take what wasn't theirs
- ♥ Gaslit, broken, and their truth erased while they were at their most vulnerable
- ♥ Hated, harassed, and purposefully pressured into giving up on who they are because of others' jealousy
- ♥ Trying to process trauma to speak in a language that isn't being heard
- ♥ Eagerly isolated by loved ones on the advice of others who can't understand them any more
- ♥ Neglected by those whose promises dimmed when things got difficult
- ♥ Treated as outcasts by those who expect their will to be done
- ♥ Mocked for what they do just because it is different and does not fit into any box

9 789349 117822

Printed at Repro India Ltd.